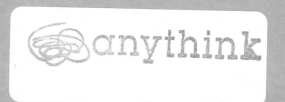

BEN RIDES ON

by MATT DAVIES

A NEAL PORTER BOOK
ROARING BROOK PRESS
NEW YORK

In books, kids can do crazy things, like haul Adrian Underbite up a cliff
and ride a bicycle without protecting their heads. In real life, you should
always remember to wear your helmet when riding your bike.

A Neal Porter Book
Published by Roaring Brook Press
Roaring Brook Press is a division of Holtzbrinck Publishing Holdings Limited Partnership
175 Fifth Avenue, New York, New York 10010
mackids.com

Library of Congress Cataloging-in-Publication Data
Ben rides on / Matt Davies. — 1st ed.
    p. cm.
    "A Neal Porter Book."
    Summary: Ben rides his new bicycle the very, very long way to school
but Adrian Underbite, perhaps the world's largest third-grader, takes the
bike anyway and later, when Ben finds Adrian in trouble, he must decide
whether or not to help the larcenous bully.
ISBN 978-1-59643-794-4 (hardcover)
[1. Bullies—Fiction. 2. Bicycles and bicycling—Fiction. 3.
Stealing—Fiction. 4. Conduct of life—Fiction.] I. Title.
    PZ7.D283825Ben 2013
    [E]—dc23
                            2012013101

Roaring Brook Press books are available for special promotions and premiums.
For details contact: Director of Special Markets, Holtzbrinck Publishers.

First edition 2013
Printed in China by Macmillan Production (Asia) Ltd., Kowloon Bay, Hong Kong (supplier code 10)

10 9 8 7 6 5 4 3 2 1

Photo courtesy Jo Thompson

For Ben

Now that he had the
bicycle of his dreams,
Ben Lukin loved
going to school.

With his gleaming new machine
he could take the long way.

Or, perhaps,
the very long way.

And maybe even the very, very long way.

It was arriving
at school that
Ben hated.

Sadly, Adrian Underbite, perhaps the world's largest third-grader, didn't seem to like Ben very much.

But Adrian did like nice things.

After watching Adrian ride off on his prized possession, Ben was devastated (and late for class).

As his teacher explained that the Earth revolved around the Sun, Ben's thoughts revolved around his bike and seeking revenge against Adrian.

When the school bell finally rang,
Ben began his journey home on foot.
He hadn't gone far when he heard a very peculiar sound . . .

which caused him to launch
an immediate investigation.

WWWGGRRAAAWWWWWRR

Whereupon, he quickly discovered
his stolen bike.

And also

Adrian . . .

who appeared to be
in a significant spot of trouble.

"How extraordinarily terrible,"
Ben thought to himself.

Ben dusted off the bent-up bicycle and continued on his way, satisfied that Adrian would perilously dangle from a tree branch for all eternity.

But something
made him stop.

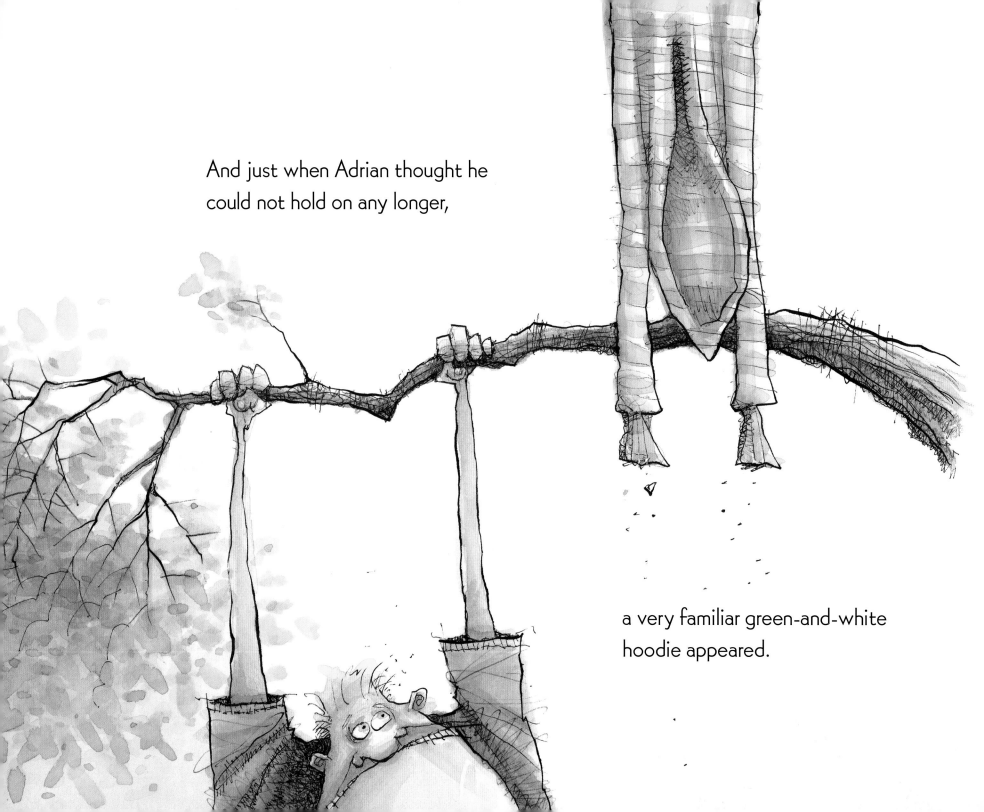

And just when Adrian thought he could not hold on any longer,

a very familiar green-and-white hoodie appeared.

Adrian reached up and
grabbed on for dear life.

Hauling the big galoot
proved to be a challenge,

but Ben pulled Adrian to safety
(with some help from a friend).

Exhausted, Adrian slowly rose
to his size ten feet

and appeared, momentarily,
to be quite puzzled.

Then suddenly, without warning, he lunged like an airborne walrus toward his rescuer.

While Ben braced for
the horrible impact . . .

Adrian made off with the damaged bike.

Ben couldn't believe it.

Worn out and feeling a bit sick,
he turned and headed for home.

Ben didn't get much
sleep that night.

The following morning, he still
had only one thing on
his mind . . .

The very thing that someone
had carefully leaned against
his front gate.

And it had been repaired,
almost perfectly.